The children went to pick
blackberries.

There were lots of blackberries. The
bushes had thorns.

"Mind the thorns," called Wilma.
"Ow!" said Chip. "The thorns are
sharp."

Wilma saw some big blackberries. She had some thick gloves and some clippers.

Wilma put on the thick gloves. She
cut the stems with the clippers.

The children went home. They ate
some blackberries.
"Yuk! This isn't ripe," said Biff.

Biff picked up the magic key. It began
to glow.
"The magic is working," said Biff.

The magic took them to a castle.
"Wow! Look at these thorns," said
Kipper.

A man was stuck in the thorns.
"Ow! Help!" he called. "I can't get free."

Wilma put on the gloves. She got the clippers. Then she cut the man free.

"Thanks," said the man. "I wanted to get to the castle, but I got stuck in the thorns."

"I am a prince," said the man. "I need to get in the castle. There is a princess in there."

"We can help," said Wilma. "We can
lend you these clippers."

The thorns were sharp but the prince
cut a way in.
"Mind the thorns," he called.

At last, they got to the castle. The prince pushed the door open.

They went inside the castle. Everyone was fast asleep.

There was dust on everything.
"Yuk!" said Kipper. "Look at the
cobwebs."

There were cobwebs everywhere. There were even cobwebs on the people.

At last, they found the princess. She
was fast asleep.
"Now what do I do?" said the prince.

"You kiss the princess," said Kipper.
"Then she wakes up. Everyone knows
that!"

The prince kissed the princess.
"Yuk," said Chip.
The princess woke up.

"At last!" said the princess.
Everyone in the castle woke up.

The magic key glowed.
"Time to go," said Biff. "The prince
doesn't need us now."

The magic adventure was over. Dad
was fast asleep.
"He's no Sleeping Beauty!" said Biff.

For Niki

The Mitten

Copyright © 1964 by Lothrop, Lee & Shepard
Printed in the United States of America.
First Mulberry Edition, 1989.   6 7 8 9 10

Library of Congress Cataloging-in-Publication Data
Tresselt, Alvin R.
The mitten : an old Ukrainian folktale /
retold by Alvin Tresselt ; illustrations by Yaroslava ;
adapted from the version by E. Rachov.
p. cm.
Reprint. Originally published: New York
: Lothrop, Lee & Shepard, 1964.
Summary: A retelling of the traditional
tale of how a boy's lost mitten becomes a refuge
from the cold for an increasing number of animals.
[1. Folklore—ukraine.]   I. Yaroslava, pseud., ill.
II. Rukavychka.   III. Title.   PZ8.1.T7Mi 1989
398.21'0947'71—dc20
[E]   89-9394   CIP   AC

An Old Ukrainian Folktale

the **M**itten

Retold by Alvin Tresselt

Illustrations by Yaroslava

Adapted from the version by E. Rachev

A MULBERRY PAPERBACK BOOK
New York

It was the coldest day of the winter,
and a little boy was trudging through the forest
gathering firewood for his grandmother.
"Bring back all you can find," the old woman had said
as she sat knitting a pair of mittens.
"The north wind blows cold, and we must have
a good fire to keep us warm."

All morning the boy worked, picking up sticks,
until his sled was well loaded.
Then a very strange thing happened.
Just as he picked up the last stick
he dropped one of his mittens in the snow.

Now, how a boy could do this
on the coldest day of winter
I'll never know, but that's the way
my grandfather tells the story.

Off he went with his load of wood,
and the mitten was left lying on a snowdrift.

As soon as he was out of sight a little mouse
came scurrying through the woods.
She was very cold, and when she spied the little boy's mitten
with its feathery fur cuff, she popped right in to get warm.
It was just the right size for a tiny mouse.

Presently a green frog came hip-hopping over the snow.
"Anybody home?" she asked when she saw the mitten.
"Only me," said the mouse, "and come in quickly
before you freeze."

They had no sooner settled themselves snugly
in the red wool lining when an owl flew down.
"May I join you in that lovely mitten?" he asked.
"If you mind your manners," replied the mouse,
for owls always made her nervous.
"And don't wiggle around too much," added the frog,
"because it's a bit tight in here."

It wasn't long before a rabbit came down the forest path.
"Is there room for me in that nice warm mitten?"
asked the rabbit. "It's awfully cold out here."
"Not much space left," said the mouse
and the frog and the owl.
"But come in. We'll see what we can do."

Even before the rabbit had gotten herself tucked in,
a fox trotted up to the mitten,
and after a good deal of trouble
she got herself in along with the others.
The mouse was beginning to think
maybe she shouldn't have been so generous,
but with the bitter wind outside, what else could she do?

And now, as if things weren't bad enough,
the next visitor was a big gray wolf
who wanted to come in, too.
"I don't know how we'll manage it," said the mouse,
"But we'll try."
Everyone moved around a bit, and finally the wolf
was squeezed into the mitten.
It was very crowded by now,
but at least it was warm.

Things had just gotten arranged nicely
when the animals heard a great snorting.
It was a wild boar, and he was very anxious
to get in out of the wind.
"Oh, dear!" cried the mouse, for the mitten
was already beginning to stretch a little.
"We just don't have any more room!"

"I'll be very careful," said the boar.
With that he squinched himself into the mitten
along with the mouse and the frog,
the owl, the rabbit, the fox and the wolf.
I know this is so because my grandfather told me.

But the worst was yet to come,
for who should appear now but a bear!
He was very big and very cold.
"No room! No room!" cried the animals
even before the bear had a chance to speak.

"Nonsense!" said the bear.
"There's always room for one more."
And, without so much as a please or thank you,
he began crawling into the mitten.
He put his paw in first, and the mitten creaked and groaned.
He put his other paw in and one of the seams popped.
Then he took a big breath and pushed himself in.

Now while all this was going on,
along came a little black cricket.
She was very old, and her creaky legs ached with the cold.
When she saw the mitten she said to herself,
"Now that looks like a nice warm place.
I'll just hop over and see if I can squeeze in, too!"

But, ah me, that's all that was needed
to finish off the poor old mitten.
The cricket had no more than put
her first scratchy foot inside when,
with a rip and a snap, the stitches came apart,
the old leather cracked
and the soft red lining split in half,
popping all the animals into the snow!

Well, at this very moment the little boy
discovered that he had only one mitten,
so back he went to see where he might have dropped the other one.
But all he could find were the ripped-apart pieces.
And he thought he saw a little mouse scurrying away
with a bit of red wool perched on her head.
It looked very much like the lining
from the thumb of his missing mitten.

"Oh, well," said the boy as he snuggled his cold hand
inside his coat, "my grandmother will surely have
my new mittens finished by now."

Then he hurried home, with the north wind
nipping at his cheeks.

And my grandfather says he never did know
what *really* happened to his mitten.